The Hungry Giant

Lee Davis

Illustrated by Colin Paine

FAMILY LEARNING

Once upon a time, there was a giant who loved food.

The giant stole all his food from the farms.

The farmers were angry with him.

"What shall we do?"
the farmers asked.

"I will give him this book," said one farmer. "It may help."

Eat Less
Get Stronger
DK

The giant looked at the book.

"I will try this," he said.

So, the giant had fruit for breakfast

and a bowl of soup for his lunch.

He had fish and

a green salad for his supper.

He drank only water.
Soon there was nothing left.

The farmers were even more angry with him.

"What shall we do?"
the farmers asked.

"I will give him this book," said one farmer. "It's about running."

"I will try this," the giant said.

So, the giant ran and ran and ran.

And the farmers never saw him again.

Picture Words

giant

food

farm

farmer

book

fruit

soup

fish

green salad

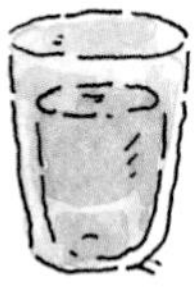

water